Pumpkin Patch Murders

THE AUTUMNBORO MYSTERIES: SMALL TOWN CHARM. BIG TIME SECRETS
BOOK ONE

BEATRICE L HOLLOWAY

Contents

1. A Harvest of Hints — 1
2. A Carved-Up Crime Scene — 5
3. Pumpkin Pie and Premonitions — 9
4. Secrets in the Stalks — 13
5. Broomsticks & Betrayal — 16
6. The Corn Maze Clue — 19
7. Grave Matters — 23
8. Midnight at the Hayride — 27
9. Apple Cider Alibis — 31
10. Trick or Trap — 35
11. The Killer Unmasked — 39
12. Falling Leaves and Fresh Starts — 43

A Harvest of Hints

If Autumnboro had a scent, it would be cinnamon-spiced apple cider with a suspicious hint of mischief.

Hazel Greene pushed open the door of her vintage orange Beetle and stepped into a world of golden leaves, scarecrow decorations, and the unmistakable tang of October. The morning fog still clung to the tops of the cornstalks that framed Wicker's Hollow Pumpkin Farm, giving the place the look of a storybook illustration—if the illustrator had a slightly sinister sense of humor.

She adjusted her oversized knit scarf, the one with tiny jack-o'-lanterns embroidered along the edge, and squinted toward the barn where she was supposed to set up her library's "Books & Boos" booth. This was Hazel's fourth year setting up shop at the Harvest Moon Festival, and while she had every intention of promoting ghost stories and fall poetry, her true mission was much simpler: people-watching and pumpkin donuts.

"You're late," called a familiar voice, warm and honeyed with just a splash of sass.

Hazel turned to see Tilly Rose, her best friend since middle school and the town's unofficial queen of baked goods, approaching with two steaming cups of cider. Her auburn curls were tucked beneath a plaid beret, and flour dusted her navy-blue cardigan like a proud badge of honor.

"I'm fashionably autumnal," Hazel countered, grinning as she accepted the drink. "And I see you brought a bribe."

Tilly winked. "Only way to make sure you don't disappear into the corn maze looking for 'literary inspiration' again."

Hazel took a sip. "One time. I got lost *one* time."

"That was three years ago and you came back quoting *Wuthering Heights* and demanding hot chocolate like a Victorian ghost."

Hazel was about to retort when the low rumble of a pickup truck cut through the air. It came to a dusty stop beside the barn, and out stepped Caleb.

Tall, broad-shouldered, and shadowed in mystery, Caleb had only been in town for a few weeks, but he'd already been dubbed "The Pumpkin Prince" by a gaggle of teenage girls at the library. He was polite, brooding, and—if Hazel was being honest—a little *too* quiet for her taste.

Caleb nodded their way. "Ladies."

"Morning, Caleb," Tilly said with a coy smile.

Hazel offered a wave, trying not to ogle. He moved with the kind of unbothered grace that made her suspicious. No one that handsome and good with hay bales was *just* a farmhand.

Before she could voice that thought, the barn doors creaked open, and out hobbled Ned Wicker, the farm's longtime owner and resident town grump. His scowl was as perennial as his pumpkins.

"Greene!" he barked. "You brought those haunted books of yours again?"

"They're just stories, Mr. Wicker," Hazel replied sweetly. "And only mildly cursed."

He grunted. "Long as they don't scare off paying customers. We need full turnout this year. Festival's barely holding steady."

Hazel exchanged a look with Tilly. That was new. Ned never worried about turnout. Wicker's Hollow was a town staple, its pumpkin patch practically sacred. Something in his tone sent a tiny chill down Hazel's spine, and it wasn't just the crisp fall breeze.

"Everything okay, Mr. Wicker?" she asked.

He glanced at Caleb, then back at Hazel, his jaw clenched. "Fine. Just fine."

Which meant, of course, that it wasn't.

Before Hazel could press him, the telltale crunch of boots on gravel drew their attention to the entrance. Sheriff Eli Marsh had arrived, coffee in hand, badge gleaming against his worn leather jacket. He was as gruff as Ned but a lot easier on the eyes.

"Morning, folks," Eli called. "Thought I'd do a walk-through before the big rush."

"You mean before the cider kicks in and someone starts a pie fight?" Hazel teased.

He chuckled, eyes landing on her with a smirk. "Wouldn't be the Harvest Moon Festival without a little chaos."

Hazel smiled, but something behind the sheriff caught her eye—a large, half-carved jack-o'-lantern, perched awkwardly at the far edge of the field, away from the others. It hadn't been there yesterday when she scouted the site, and it looked oddly... slumped. Like it had been placed there in a hurry. Or to be hidden.

She took a step toward it, the hairs on her arms prickling beneath her sweater.

"Hazel?" Tilly asked. "You okay?"

Hazel narrowed her eyes at the strange pumpkin. "Yeah. Just... something about that one."

Caleb followed her gaze. "Don't worry about that," he said quickly. "I'll take care of it."

But something in his tone made Hazel pause. It was too quick. Too rehearsed.

She tilted her head. "Looks like it's leaking."

A thin, dark trail was oozing from the jack-o'-lantern's crooked grin, seeping into the soil.

It wasn't pumpkin guts.

It was red.

Hazel's breath hitched. A gust of wind swept through the field, making the corn whisper and the scarecrows shiver. Somewhere in the distance, a crow let out a sharp caw.

The cider in her stomach turned.

"Tilly," she said, her voice tight. "Does that look like... blood to you?"

A Carved-Up Crime Scene

The sun had barely cleared the treetops when Hazel Greene turned off the road and onto the winding gravel drive of Wicker's Hollow Pumpkin Farm. The fog hadn't lifted yet. It clung low to the ground like a whisper that didn't want to be heard, curling around the stalks and creeping across the field like it had secrets to keep.

She parked her Beetle beneath the old sycamore, grabbed her box of decorations, and stepped into the eerie stillness. No crows. No farmhands. Just the soft crunch of her boots and the faint creak of the barn's weather vane spinning in the breeze.

Hazel shivered. She'd been on this farm a hundred times over the years, but this morning it felt different—like the very earth was holding its breath.

"I do not scare easily," she muttered. "I shelve horror novels for a living."

Still, she moved a little faster toward the main barn, where she was planning to finish setting up the Books & Boos booth. But something pulled her gaze back to the field. Something large. Something orange.

The jack-o'-lantern.

It was still there, at the far edge of the pumpkin rows—maybe ten feet wide and grotesquely grinning, its carved smile jagged and crooked. Hazel paused, squinting. Had it... moved?

She stepped off the path and into the patch, the dewy grass soaking her ankles. As she neared the enormous pumpkin, her heart ticked up. Something was wrong with it. The air around it smelled off—sweet and rotting, but also metallic. Coppery.

The box of decorations slipped from her grip and hit the ground with a soft thud.

Hazel knelt beside the pumpkin, her fingers trembling slightly as she reached toward the jagged grin. A flash of red caught her eye—fabric. Velvet.

And then... she saw it.

A hand, limp and pale, emerging from inside the pumpkin. Fingers curled unnaturally, nails painted a bright, unforgiving pink. Just below the wrist, a broken charm bracelet dangled, one golden apple charm missing.

Hazel staggered back, one hand clamped over her mouth.

"Oh no... oh no no no..."

It was a body.

More than a body—it was Cora Belle.

Hazel recognized the gaudy jewelry and the red velvet shawl she wore to nearly every public event. Her face was partially visible through the carved mouth, a grotesque parody of a grin stretched across her features. Her eyes, glassy and half-lidded, stared into nothing.

Hazel stumbled away, yanking her phone from her coat pocket. Her fingers barely worked, but she managed to hit speed dial.

"Sheriff Marsh," came the sleepy voice on the other end.

"It's Hazel. You need to come to the pumpkin farm. Now. It's Cora. She's—" Hazel swallowed, "She's dead."

Sheriff Eli Marsh arrived fifteen minutes later, still buttoning up his jacket, his boots kicking up gravel as he rushed across the field. One look at Hazel's face, and he stopped short.

"She's in there?" he asked grimly, nodding toward the jack-o'-lantern.

Hazel nodded, her arms crossed tightly. "Inside it. Like... someone stuffed her in there."

Eli ducked beneath the crooked smile and stepped back just as quickly. "Holy hell."

Deputy Lyle soon followed, and the two men began cordoning off the area with old yellow caution tape pulled from the trunk of the cruiser. It looked pitiful against the backdrop of hay bales and festively painted signs.

Tilly arrived next, breathless and pale, a paper bag of pumpkin scones clutched in her arms like a talisman. She took one look at Hazel's face, then at the scene behind her, and gasped.

"Cora? No. Are you sure?"

Hazel didn't answer. She didn't need to.

"Could've been an accident," Sheriff Marsh said an hour later as he jotted something in his notebook.

Hazel blinked. "Excuse me?"

"I mean... she could've passed out. Maybe had a heart attack out here, and someone panicked. Tried to hide it."

Hazel stared at him. "In a jack-o'-lantern?"

Eli looked mildly sheepish. "Well. It's a big pumpkin."

She took a deep breath. "No one *accidentally* ends up dead inside a carved gourd, Eli. She was shoved in there."

He rubbed his jaw. "I don't disagree. But we don't have proof of anything criminal. Yet."

Hazel pointed to the bracelet still clinging to Cora's wrist. "That charm bracelet? It's broken. One of the charms is missing."

"And?"

"And maybe whoever killed her tore it off."

Marsh glanced at the scene again, brow furrowing. "Let the coroner take a look first. We'll know more soon."

Hazel bit her tongue. Barely.

She glanced down at the dirt near the pumpkin. A few smudged boot prints trailed off toward the edge of the field. Not farm boots. Not work boots. Too small. And yet no one seemed to care.

. . .

By the time the sun was high in the sky, the festival grounds were swarming with whispers. People clutched cider cups like life preservers and avoided the far end of the field, where the jack-o'-lantern still loomed like a twisted Halloween monument.

Hazel sat on a bench outside Tilly's bakery, sipping strong black coffee and ignoring the library flyers in her bag.

"Cora had enemies," Tilly said quietly. "Half the town hated her, and the other half just tolerated her for the sake of the Harvest Queen contest."

"She was festival royalty," Hazel muttered. "And someone made her into the centerpiece."

Tilly frowned. "You really think it was murder?"

"I *know* it."

Hazel stared out the bakery window toward the distant outline of the pumpkin farm.

"And I'm going to find out who carved her into that display."

"That pumpkin wasn't carved for fun," Hazel murmured to the empty room. *"It was carved for a warning."*

Pumpkin Pie and Premonitions

The bell above Sweet Bakes Bakery jingled its familiar tune as Hazel stepped inside, carrying the scent of cinnamon, crisp air, and quiet determination with her. The warm aroma of nutmeg, cloves, and caramel hit her like a hug. If there was one place in Autumnboro that could soften the edges of a murder investigation, it was Tilly Rose's kitchen.

Hazel hadn't slept much. Every time she closed her eyes, she saw that jack-o'-lantern grin again—Cora's lifeless eyes staring through the carved mouth like she was warning the whole town from beyond.

Tilly popped up from behind the counter, her curls tied back with a black-and-orange bandana, flour streaking her cheek like war paint.

"I saved you the best slice," she said without preamble.

"You're a saint," Hazel sighed, slumping into their usual corner booth by the window.

"Saint of pastries, maybe." Tilly joined her with two steaming mugs of coffee and two generous slices of pumpkin pie. "Figured you could use something warm, sweet, and heavily spiced after yesterday's nightmare."

Hazel stared at the pie for a beat. "Do you think Cora would've appreciated being found in a pumpkin?"

Tilly made a face. "Hazel."

"I'm serious. She always wanted to be the center of attention."

"She wanted to be Harvest Queen until the day she died. Just not in a gourd."

Hazel managed a thin smile and took a bite. The pie was perfect—smooth, rich, just the right amount of bite to the spice. It steadied her enough to speak what had been tumbling in her mind all night.

"Something's off about all this," she said, nudging her pie crust with a fork. "Sheriff Marsh is writing it off like a freak accident, but Cora Belle didn't just fall into a jack-o'-lantern and die."

"No," Tilly agreed, lowering her voice. "She got stuffed in there. Like a scarecrow no one wanted to look at too closely."

"And that bracelet she was wearing? The charm was broken. It was her favorite one. A gold apple. I've seen her flash it like a badge when she's trying to look more important."

"I remember. Didn't she say it was a gift from someone 'special'?"

"She said that about every piece of jewelry she owned." Hazel leaned in. "But I asked around this morning. Apparently, she told Judy over at the flower shop that she was going to expose someone this week."

Tilly raised her brows. "Expose? That's serious language for a woman whose biggest scandal last year was smuggling extra cinnamon sticks from the community pantry."

"Judy said she was being cryptic. Something about 'knowing too much' and how someone would 'pay the price.'"

"That sounds a lot like blackmail."

"Exactly."

"So who was she threatening?"

Hazel tilted her head, thinking. "We know she had run-ins with Mayor Pickens. There was that argument during last month's council meeting."

"I heard she accused him of skimming funds from the festival's budget."

"And what about Ned Wicker?" Hazel added. "He's been acting cagey. The farm's been in his family for three generations, and now suddenly he's worried about ticket sales?"

"You don't think he's the killer, do you?"

"I think a lot of people might've wanted Cora gone. She was nosy, manipulative, and always sniffing around secrets."

Tilly took another bite of pie, chewing thoughtfully. "So, what's your plan, Miss Greene?"

"I'm going to ask a few questions. Nothing serious. Just... friendly conversations. Some light investigating."

"You mean snooping."

"Research. I'm a librarian, after all. I specialize in gathering information."

"You specialize in Dewey Decimal and overdue fines. This is murder."

"I'm just helping. It's not like I'm going to confront a killer. I'm just... connecting the dots."

Tilly sighed and pushed a second slice of pie her way. "If you're going to stick your nose in other people's business, you'd better keep it full of sugar and cinnamon."

"That's the spirit."

Hazel returned to the library later that afternoon and holed up in the local history archives, flipping through old town records and newspaper clippings. The familiar smell of old paper and binding glue soothed her nerves, sharpening her focus. She found a few interesting tidbits tucked away in the archives. Cora Belle had once sued the Wicker farm over a "trip-and-fall" near the hayride path. She lost, but the case had been messy. She had also penned strongly worded letters to the local paper accusing the mayor's office of hiding festival funds.

And perhaps most interesting of all: Cora had a late-night meeting scheduled the night before she died, according to the festival volunteer sign-in sheet. The signature was barely legible, smudged beyond recognition. But someone had met her. That was certain.

Hazel copied everything into her notebook, each page filling with scribbles, theories, and underlined names. By the time the sun dipped behind the hills and the wind whispered through the branches outside the library, she had a working list of suspects—and a sense that this mystery was only beginning to unravel.

She stood at her kitchen window that night, sipping tea and staring out at the jack-o'-lanterns she'd placed on the porch earlier in the week. Their grins didn't seem so cheerful anymore.

She tapped her pen against the page, rereading the last line she'd written: *Cora knew something. She threatened the wrong person. And now she's silent.*

Hazel closed the book gently and turned off the porch light.

Something across the street caught her eye. A figure. Just at the edge of the pumpkin patch beyond her neighbor's fence. Still. Watching.

She blinked.

But it was already gone.

Secrets in the Stalks

By Saturday morning, the festival was in full swing—and Hazel was already on her third cider of the day.

The booths were bustling, the hayrides were rolling, and the townsfolk, ever resilient, seemed determined to enjoy the Harvest Moon Festival despite the jack-o'-lantern-shaped shadow hanging over it. Still, the air felt different. Not just chilly, but heavy, like the whole town was waiting for something to happen—and pretending it wasn't.

Hazel wove through the booths with a notebook in one pocket and cinnamon sugar on her sleeve. The aroma of roasted nuts and kettle corn mingled with the sharp scent of hay and woodsmoke. Kids ran between rows of cornstalks with painted faces, clutching pumpkin balloons, while parents lingered with cider and gossip.

And oh, the gossip was *thick* today.

At the candied apple stand, Hazel overheard two local teens whispering about the "Pumpkin Body." One claimed Cora Belle's ghost had already been spotted near the hayride. The other said her spirit was trapped inside the giant jack-o'-lantern and would curse anyone who took a selfie with it.

At the craft booth, a retired schoolteacher murmured to her friend that Cora had been seen arguing with **someone in the mayor's office** a week ago—"and not about budget cuts, if you catch my drift."

But it was at the face-painting tent that Hazel caught something truly interesting. A pair of festival vendors were leaning close, speaking in hushed tones as they painted bat wings on a giggling toddler.

"I heard she had a *lover*," one said, dipping her brush in glitter. "Someone married."

"No, no," the other replied, "I heard she was seeing someone much younger. And Ned Wicker knew. That's why the farm's in trouble."

Hazel slowed her pace, pretending to examine a rack of crocheted scarves. Her heart gave a small, excited thump.

A lover. A secret. A motive?

She finished her cider and turned toward the library. If there was one place secrets liked to hide, it was between the yellowing pages of a forgotten file.

The archives were quiet—dusty and still, as if the room knew she was looking for something it didn't want her to find. Hazel pulled out the box labeled *Autumnboro Festivals, 2005–2010* and began flipping through old flyers, receipts, and volunteer rosters. Then, tucked between a stack of Harvest Queen entry forms, she found it: a photo, faded and curled at the corners.

It was from the 2007 Harvest Moon Festival. A younger **Ned Wicker** stood in front of the old hayride cart, his arm wrapped tightly around a smiling, glamorous **Cora Belle**.

They weren't just posing for a picture. They were *close*. His hand rested on her hip. Her head leaned against his shoulder. They looked, Hazel thought, like two people with a shared secret.

She studied it for a long moment, then slipped it into her notebook. That could explain Ned's twitchiness. And maybe even his sudden desperation about festival attendance. Was Cora threatening to tell someone? His family? The town?

Back at the farm, Hazel made her way to the corn maze.

It towered around her like a forest of golden walls. Children ran past her, giggling, their feet crunching over the dirt paths. But Hazel wasn't here for fun. She was looking for **Caleb**.

She found him near the south entrance, stacking bales of hay with practiced ease. He didn't smile when he saw her. Just nodded, and kept working.

"Busy morning?" Hazel asked, casually.

"Festival's picking up," he replied.

She let the silence stretch for a moment, then: "You knew Cora, didn't you?"

His hands paused mid-lift.

"I met her," he said flatly.

"She seemed to know you. Or at least, she knew *of* you. Did she ever mention Ned? Or the farm?"

He gave her a long, unreadable look. "Why are you asking?"

Hazel stepped closer, keeping her voice soft. "Because someone murdered her. And she was clearly keeping secrets."

Caleb dropped the bale with a heavy thud.

"I don't know anything about that," he said, voice tense. "She was always talking. Always stirring things up. You poke the wrong people in this town, eventually you get what's coming."

Hazel's breath caught. "That sounds a little harsh."

"Doesn't mean it's not true."

He turned and walked off toward the barn, leaving Hazel standing there, alone among the cornstalks.

She glanced at the path into the maze, now quiet and empty.

She didn't believe in ghosts.

But when she stepped into the corn, a shiver ran down her spine.

The air shifted.

A whisper, like rustling skirts and secrets not meant to be heard, seemed to follow her in.

Broomsticks & Betrayal

By Monday morning, Autumnboro had officially decided to pretend it wasn't haunted by a murder.

The Harvest Moon Festival committee posted a chipper announcement on social media that the Halloween parade would proceed as planned, the pumpkin pie contest would take place at noon sharp, and all costume-related drama would be left to the fictional ghosts, goblins, and ghouls.

Hazel Greene wasn't surprised.

If there was one thing this town knew how to do, it was sweep things under a doily and pretend it was decoration.

The town hall was packed that evening, the old wooden chairs creaking under the weight of nerves and concealed grudges. Hazel took her usual spot near the back, notebook balanced on her knee, pen poised like a wand. Her instincts were sharper than ever, and they all pointed to one thing: the murderer was here.

Cora Belle's name was not mentioned until twenty-three minutes into the meeting, and even then it came from **Eunice Greggs**, who clearly hadn't read the unspoken town script.

"Are we really going to pretend one of the festival judges wasn't *stuffed into a pumpkin* like a rotting pie filling?" Eunice snapped, arms crossed over her oversized cauldron sweater.

An uncomfortable ripple spread through the room like cold tea spilled on a tablecloth.

Mayor Pickens cleared his throat. "The investigation is ongoing, and out of respect, I think it's best we move forward with the festival and honor Cora's memory—"

"Honor?" Eunice barked a laugh. "Cora Belle made enemies in this room. Half of you wanted her gone."

A sharp intake of breath from the front row. Someone dropped their travel mug.

Hazel scanned the room. There was **Ned Wicker**, arms folded tightly, face unreadable. **Caleb** stood near the exit, leaning against the wall like he wanted to disappear into it. The mayor's assistant, **Gail**, kept scribbling notes in her agenda, but her hand was shaking.

"I'm not saying she deserved it," Eunice continued, quieter now. "But we all know she was poking around in other people's business. She made threats. Accused the mayor of stealing. Said Ned's farm was failing. That Tilly's cinnamon rolls were made with margarine, for heaven's sake!"

Hazel caught Tilly's indignant gasp from across the aisle.

Mayor Pickens banged his gavel. "That's enough. This is not a witch hunt."

Wrong choice of words.

Hazel swore she felt the air shift. Goosebumps prickled her arms.

The rest of the meeting passed in tense silence, with no resolution except this: Halloween was going ahead, the festival would be festive, and anyone who didn't like it could stay home and hand out raisins.

Hazel stayed behind as people filed out, her thoughts turning over like dead leaves in wind.

Outside, the wind had picked up. The jack-o'-lanterns lining Main Street flickered behind their grins. She passed the bakery—dark now, shutters drawn. Passed the pumpkin patch, where the stalks rustled like whispers. And finally reached the **Autumnboro Public Library**, her sanctuary.

The moment she stepped inside, she sensed it—something was off.

The scent was different. Not the usual blend of old books and paper. It was sharper. Coppery. Familiar.

Hazel slowly crossed the front room, the only light coming from the green glow of the desk lamp she'd left on earlier. She should've turned around, called the sheriff, waited outside.

But she didn't.

She moved deeper into the stacks.

That's when she saw it—just a flicker.

A shape.

A shadow.

A flash of movement between shelves.

Hazel's heart thundered. She turned toward the noise—barely a whisper—and there it was.

A figure. Cloaked in black.

Witch's hat tilted.

Long, dark robes swaying.

They moved swiftly down the reference aisle.

Hazel followed—just fast enough to see a flick of the cloak disappear through the staff door.

She pushed through it just as it banged shut behind whoever had been inside, but when she looked around the staff hallway, it was empty.

No footprints. No costume. No sign of entry or exit.

Hazel locked the door behind her, heart in her throat, then checked the archives. Nothing missing—except her notebook.

She stood still, listening to her own breath.

Then she turned back to the front desk.

There, on her keyboard, sat a single charm.

A tiny gold apple.

The Corn Maze Clue

Wicker's Hollow had always been charming during the day—sunlight filtering through the amber leaves, pumpkins smiling from every porch, the scent of hay and cider hanging like a friendly fog. But once the sun dipped below the treetops and the light bled out of the sky, the charm twisted into something else entirely.

Hazel Greene stood at the edge of the corn maze, her breath a faint plume in the cold night air. The maze looked different after dark. Larger. Wilder. Like the stalks had grown an inch just to watch her squirm.

She hadn't told anyone she was coming back here. Not even Tilly. If she had, there would've been a whole lecture about "not becoming the second body in a jack-o'-lantern." But Hazel couldn't shake the feeling that Cora's murder had roots deeper than anyone realized—and those roots were buried somewhere in this field.

With one last glance behind her, she clicked on her phone flashlight and stepped into the maze.

The corn closed in quickly, tall and tight and whispering with each movement of the wind. The dirt path beneath her boots was dry and crunching. She passed a few faded arrows pointing in different directions—some twisted, others obscured by the stalks. The maze hadn't been maintained in a few days, and it felt almost abandoned now, more haunted house than wholesome attraction.

As she made her way deeper, Hazel noticed the silence. No laughter from kids. No rustling from volunteers in scarecrow costumes. Just her footsteps and the occasional creak of corn bending somewhere just out of sight.

Then something snagged on the edge of her boot.

She stopped.

A strip of red velvet, torn and fluttering slightly, was tangled at the base of a stalk.

Hazel bent down and gently pulled it free. The fabric was soft and unmistakable. Cora's shawl. She recognized the color immediately—deep garnet red, dramatic, and always draped like she was walking a runway at all times.

A chill threaded down Hazel's spine.

She scanned the dirt path with her light and spotted something else. A small crumple of paper, wedged beneath a crooked stalk that had clearly been stepped on. She carefully lifted it, noting the creases and the smudged edge, like someone had held it too tightly. Or in a panic.

The message was written in harsh, hurried strokes.

"You should've kept your mouth shut, Cora.

Now you'll be part of the harvest."

Hazel's stomach flipped. Her flashlight flickered.

The sound came next—barely audible, a soft shuffle through the corn, like someone dragging a rake just out of sight.

She froze. Held her breath.

Was it wind?

Or footsteps?

Hazel straightened slowly, her heartbeat thudding in her ears. She tucked the note and fabric scrap into her coat pocket and began retracing her steps—but now, the path looked... unfamiliar.

Had she come from the left or the right fork?

Her phone buzzed.

A message from Tilly: *Where are you? You okay?*

Hazel started typing a response, but the moment her fingers touched the screen, she heard another sound—closer this time. The sharp *crack* of a stalk snapping underfoot. She spun around, flashlight raised.

"Hello?" she called. Her voice came out smaller than she intended.

No answer.

Another crack.

Hazel turned and bolted.

She ran through the twisting maze, breath hitching, the flashlight bobbing with every step. Panic bloomed in her chest as she realized how far in she'd gone. The signs were gone. The corners unfamiliar. She passed a fake skeleton propped against a fence post—and for a split second, it looked real.

She stumbled into a clearing where a scarecrow had been set up as part of the haunted hayride trail. It was grinning. Arms outstretched. But someone had *moved* it.

The straw hat was missing.

And around its neck... a thin strip of red velvet had been tied in a loose bow.

Hazel took a shaky breath.

That's when a beam of light cut through the maze behind her.

A voice followed, sharp and angry.

"Hazel!"

She turned. Sheriff Marsh.

He strode toward her, the flashlight in his hand revealing the pale, angry lines of his face.

"You've got to be kidding me," he growled. "What are you doing out here?"

"I found something." Hazel reached into her pocket, pulling out the velvet scrap and the crumpled note. "Look."

Marsh's expression shifted. He took the items from her hands, scanning the note.

His jaw tightened. "Where exactly did you find this?"

"By the eastern path. Near one of the dead ends. It was tucked under a stalk, like someone left it there."

"Or dropped it," Marsh muttered. "Either way, this is evidence. Which means you're now interfering with a crime scene."

"You weren't going to come back out here," Hazel said quietly. "You thought it was over."

"I thought you'd listen."

"Well, you thought wrong."

They stood in tense silence for a moment, the scarecrow watching from behind like a silent judge. Finally, Marsh pocketed the note and handed her the velvet scrap.

"Go home, Hazel. Stay out of this before someone else gets hurt."

Hazel didn't answer.

She followed him out of the maze, the corn rustling behind them like it was whispering secrets.

Her house was dark when she arrived, the porch light having burned out earlier in the week. Hazel stepped inside, locked the door behind her, and placed the velvet scrap and her notes on the kitchen table. She brewed tea with shaking hands and tried to ignore the way her eyes kept drifting to the window.

Just nerves, she told herself. Just nerves and shadows and a scarecrow that shouldn't have been wearing red.

She turned to flip off the light—

And saw something on her porch.

A small brown paper bag tied with twine.

Her hands froze around the switch.

She opened the door slowly, heart thudding. The night air poured in, colder now.

No one was there.

She brought the bag inside and untied the twine. Inside was a single slice of pumpkin pie—golden, flaky, perfect.

But someone had carved a word into the top of the crust with a paring knife.

STOP.

Hazel stared at it, the air around her going still.

And then the doorbell rang.

Grave Matters

The graveyard was nearly empty when Hazel arrived, except for the crows.

They lined the wrought-iron fence like sentries, silent and watchful, their black eyes tracking her every step. The sky hung heavy and gray, clouds thick like bruises. Hazel tightened her scarf and stepped through the old gate, boots crunching over brittle leaves and forgotten flower petals.

It was her idea to host a **spooky storytime** for the children at the library. Halloween week tradition. Costumes, apple cider, shadowy tales read aloud by flickering lanterns. And what better place to rehearse than the **Autumnboro Cemetery**, where the stories had already been written—in marble and moss.

She wandered past rows of tilted tombstones, some too weathered to read, others polished to a shine. The wind sighed through the trees, and every creaking branch sounded like a whisper.

Hazel stopped near the **Wicker family plot**. It stood near the center of the cemetery, enclosed by an old, rusted gate and overgrown with ivy. The Wickers had been in Autumnboro longer than the streets had names. Old money, older grudges.

She leaned down to brush a leaf from the nearest marker—and noticed it.

A patch of **disturbed soil**, just beside a headstone worn to the point of illegibility.

The ground had been recently dug up. Then poorly covered. No grass. No fresh flowers. Just churned earth and a thin line of powdery dust, like someone had tried to scatter something—then changed their mind.

Hazel crouched, brushing the soil back carefully with her fingers.

A corner of **something metallic** glinted in the dirt.

She hesitated. Then pulled.

Out came a **lockbox**, old and rusted, its hinges crusted with age. It was small—no bigger than a shoebox—and surprisingly heavy. There was no lock, just a sliding latch.

Hazel's breath caught. She looked around—still alone.

She opened it.

Inside was a bundle of **old letters**, tied with red ribbon now faded to a dusty rose. The pages were yellowed, but the ink remained dark, each one signed with the initials **C.B.** or **N.W.**

Cora Belle. Ned Wicker.

Hazel sat on a nearby stone bench and read.

The first letter was dated **1979**.

Ned,

If you won't acknowledge me publicly, at least give me what I'm owed. I've kept quiet for years, but your silence feels more like shame than protection. You owe me more than just visits at midnight.

—Cora

Hazel's hands trembled slightly.

The next one was even clearer.

Ned,

Your wife is not blind. She knows. She always knew. And now so does your son. If you won't give me my share of the farm, I'll go to the festival committee. Or the mayor. Or your precious church board. Don't test me.

—Cora Belle W.

W.

Hazel's heart skipped.

Belle *Wicker*?

Another letter, older still, hinted at something even darker. Talks of a pregnancy. A child. A deal made in secret.

She flipped through the bundle with increasing horror. Cora Belle hadn't just had an affair with Ned Wicker. She had likely been part of the Wicker family—*married into it*, if only briefly. And there was mention, more than once, of "the boy" and "keeping him away from the farm until he's of age."

Hazel whispered the words as they formed.

"Oh my God."

Could it be Caleb?

It made too much sense. The way Ned watched him, guarded but not unfamiliar. The way Caleb spoke about Cora, sharp and bitter but... personal.

She placed the letters back into the lockbox and glanced at the gravestone again. It was so weathered, almost blank—but with the right angle of light, she could just make out a name.

Coraline B. Wicker.

So it wasn't just gossip. It was history, buried—literally—in the family plot.

The wind picked up, hissing through the ivy like a warning. The trees swayed. Hazel stood quickly, brushing soil from her hands. She turned to leave—

And froze.

Someone was standing at the far end of the path.

Half-hidden behind the trees.

Watching.

A figure in black.

Hazel couldn't make out a face, but the silhouette was unmistakable. Tall. Still.

The same shape she'd seen from her car outside the corn maze.

She stepped forward, pulse racing. "Who's there?"

The figure didn't move.

Hazel took another step—but a sudden gust of wind howled through the cemetery, whipping her scarf around her face. When she pulled it free, the path was empty again.

She turned and ran. Out through the rusting gate, through rows of gravestones, the lockbox clutched tight to her chest.

Later that night, back in her kitchen, Hazel read through the letters again with trembling hands. Tilly sat across from her, eyes wide, a mug of untouched tea cooling in front of her.

"You're saying Cora was a Wicker? As in *part* of the Wicker family?" Tilly asked.

Hazel nodded. "And she had leverage. Real leverage. Property, bloodlines, possibly even a son."

Tilly swallowed. "And now she's dead."

Hazel leaned back in her chair, her eyes drifting to the lockbox.

"This wasn't just a murder," she said softly. "It was a cover-up."

Outside, the wind rattled the windowpanes like fingernails on glass. Hazel didn't flinch.

She was too busy trying to figure out whether the past had finally clawed its way up from the grave...

...or if it had been *pushed* out by someone desperate to keep it buried.

Midnight at the Hayride

The sky was ink-black and full of stars—bright enough to sparkle but not strong enough to chase away the shadows clinging to the edges of **Wicker's Hollow**. It was the last night of the festival's haunted hayride, and laughter echoed across the fields like echoes from another world.

Hazel Greene sat in the back of the final wagon, her breath fogging in the cool October air, eyes narrowed behind a pair of novelty bat-ear earmuffs she'd borrowed from Tilly. Around her, kids clutched bags of kettle corn while teens tried not to scream at the costumed actors leaping from the corn. Parents sipped cider and rolled their eyes.

Hazel wasn't here for the jump scares.

She was here because someone had been watching her. And tonight, she planned to watch back.

The hayride jostled down the worn trail, the wooden wheels creaking in rhythm. The actors were good—almost too good. One scarecrow lunged a little *too* close. One cloaked figure stared a little too long.

As the wagon turned near the edge of the pumpkin field, Hazel spotted movement near the barn. A figure stepped away from the shadows—tall, cloaked, and careful.

They weren't part of the hayride.

Hazel quietly climbed down from the wagon as it slowed to a stop near the cider station. No one noticed. The crowd was too busy shrieking at a man with a plastic chainsaw.

She slipped into the darkness, following the figure at a distance as they crossed toward the **old barn**, the one used for storage and rarely opened during the festival. Its doors stood slightly ajar, one creaking as the figure slipped inside.

Hazel hesitated at the threshold. She could hear the distant thump of music from the food stalls and the whistle of the wind in the trees. But in here, everything was still. Too still.

She stepped inside.

The barn smelled of hay, rusted tools, and something sour beneath it all—like old apples left to rot. Moonlight filtered through a broken window, catching on dust motes and illuminating the scattered contents: bales of hay, crates of fall decorations, and in the center...

A **scarecrow**.

Hazel paused.

It wasn't part of the hayride. She'd been on this property every day for a week—this was *new*.

It stood against the far wall, slumped slightly, a burlap sack pulled over its head, one arm dangling limp. It was oddly... human in posture. Not upright and goofy like the others. This one had been assembled with care. Too much care.

Hazel's hand hovered over her phone. Something told her to leave. But something else—stronger—pulled her forward.

She reached the scarecrow and gently touched the fabric of its shirt.

Real flannel.

The buttons were mismatched. There was dirt on the cuffs.

She stepped closer and tugged at the collar.

A glimpse of **lace** underneath. A string of plastic **pearls**.

Hazel froze.

She pulled harder—and the scarecrow's body shifted.

Something **thumped** inside the chest cavity. A solid, soft weight. Something *not* straw.

Heart pounding, Hazel grabbed the hem of the shirt and lifted it up.

Inside was a tightly packed bundle of evidence—Cora's **missing**

purse, a cracked **cell phone**, a small plastic **bag of jewelry charms**, and something even worse:

A stained **parchment envelope**, sealed with wax.

She opened it with trembling fingers.

Inside was a **photograph**—Cora and Ned Wicker, just like before, but this time the photo was newer. Cora was holding up a copy of **a will**. The name "Wicker" was written in bold at the top. Below that, just barely legible: **"amendment of inheritance."**

Hazel's mouth went dry.

She stepped back—right as the **barn door slammed shut behind her.**

She spun around.

Nothing but black.

She ran to the door, tugged—it wouldn't budge.

She pounded on the wood. "Hello? Is someone there? Let me out!"

No answer.

Then a sound behind her. A long, dragging shuffle through the hay.

Hazel turned toward the scarecrow.

It hadn't moved. But something behind it had.

She reached for her flashlight—and realized she'd dropped it. Her phone was gone too. Lost somewhere between the barn and the hayride.

She was alone. In the dark. With a scarecrow that wasn't really a scarecrow and a killer who was getting very, very close.

Hazel backed toward the window, heart hammering, eyes darting to every corner. The silence in the barn was thick now, pressing in. Then came a whisper—so faint she wasn't sure it was real.

"Should've stayed out of it..."

Hazel spun, tripped, landed hard on the hay-covered floor—and her hand landed on something cold and sharp.

A **garden trowel**.

She grabbed it, stood, and held it out like a sword. "I don't know who you are," she said into the dark, "but I'm not going down like a storybook extra."

Something moved in the rafters above.

A creak. A scuffle. Then silence.

Hazel's breath came fast. She took slow steps toward the barn wall and slammed the trowel against it in rhythm—**bang, bang, bang**—until, finally, a voice called from outside.

"Hazel?!"

Sheriff Marsh.

She rushed to the door. "I'm in here!"

Moments later, the latch lifted. Marsh pulled the door open, flashlight cutting into the gloom.

He took one look at her and the makeshift scarecrow. Then the photo in her hand.

And his face went pale.

"What did you find?" he asked.

Hazel didn't answer. She just handed him the photo.

He stared at it. Then looked up slowly, his voice low.

"You need to come with me. Now."

Hazel glanced back at the scarecrow—no longer a costume, but a warning.

The barn had tried to bury the truth.

But it was far too late for secrets now.

Apple Cider Alibis

Hazel sat at the kitchen table, her hands wrapped around a mug of cider that had long gone cold.

The barn. The scarecrow. The will.

She still couldn't shake the feeling of hay clinging to her skin, or the image of that sagging flannel-shirted figure stuffed with secrets. She hadn't slept. Not really. She'd lain awake all night with the photograph in her mind, Cora's smirk practically daring her to keep going.

Across from her, Tilly stirred sugar into her mug with a cinnamon stick, lips pressed tight. She hadn't said much since Hazel had come knocking just after dawn, looking pale, breathless, and very much like someone who'd been locked in a murder barn.

"You're telling me Cora had an amended version of Ned Wicker's will," Tilly said finally, "and it was hidden in a fake scarecrow. Inside a locked barn. That just so happens to be owned by the *mayor*?"

Hazel nodded.

Tilly exhaled through her nose. "I need something stronger than cider."

They spread Hazel's findings across the table: the photograph, the letter referencing inheritance, the torn velvet scrap, and the plastic bag of jewelry charms—some from Cora's signature bracelet, others unfamiliar. Hazel had spent the early hours matching handwriting from the old letters she'd found in the cemetery with the signature on the amendment in the photo. It matched.

And Mayor Harold Pickens? His name appeared at the bottom of the page—twice. Once in the list of witnesses. Once in the line where it said "Executor of Estate."

"What if this was never about a family feud?" Hazel whispered. "What if it was about the land?"

Tilly frowned. "You think the mayor killed her over pumpkins?"

Hazel pulled her laptop closer and opened the folder she'd saved from the town archive server.

"Mayor Pickens helped secure the zoning permits for Wicker's Hollow to expand into the backfields a few years ago. But that land used to be part of a protected woodland. There was pushback—until Cora testified in favor of the expansion."

"She hated environmental groups," Tilly said. "Said they blocked her from adding a koi pond to her backyard."

"Exactly. She backed the mayor's proposal, and in return, he promised her something."

Hazel clicked open a scanned deed from 2018.

"Look here. The barn? The land it's on? It's not technically Wicker family property anymore. It was quietly transferred to the *Autumnboro Development Trust*—which Mayor Pickens manages."

Tilly leaned closer. "So, the barn where you found the scarecrow isn't even Ned's anymore. It's Harold's."

Hazel nodded slowly. "And if Cora found out he was planning to sell that land off—or worse, that he never filed the will amendment after Ned signed it—she had leverage."

"Enough to blackmail him."

"Or threaten to expose him."

"And now she's dead."

They both stared at the documents in silence for a long moment. Then Tilly whispered, "Do you think Caleb knows?"

Hazel tapped her fingers against the mug. "I think Caleb is still hiding something. Maybe he knows about the will. Maybe he's the son referenced in those old letters. But I don't think he's the one stuffing scarecrows."

"Which leaves us with Harold." Tilly chewed her bottom lip. "If he's willing to bury Cora's amendment, what else is he hiding?"

Hazel stood and grabbed her bag.

"We're going to find out."

They headed to the **town clerk's office**, tucked inside a crooked brick building next to the post office. The clerk, Florence, was a woman with a strong sense of civic pride and an even stronger sense of boredom. But Hazel had bribed her before—with gingerbread scones and a signed copy of *The Witching Hour Book Club's* latest thriller.

Thirty minutes later, Florence wheeled out a metal cart stacked with manila folders and dusty binders.

Hazel flipped through a 2019 expense report for the festival.

"Look at this. Five thousand dollars for 'lighting upgrades' at Wicker's Hollow."

"There are no new lights," Tilly said.

"And two thousand for 'barn restoration.' The same barn."

Hazel stared down at the mayor's signature at the bottom of the page. A sharp, sweeping scrawl.

Tilly whispered, "He was laundering money through the festival budget."

Hazel nodded slowly. "And the only person who knew? Cora Belle."

She set the file down.

"It's time we pay the mayor a visit."

Tilly raised an eyebrow. "Subtle or dramatic?"

Hazel smiled grimly.

"Let's start with subtle. But bring the pie. Just in case."

That night, Hazel lay awake again. The cider had gone untouched. Her thoughts were racing, faster than before. If Mayor Pickens had manipulated the will, stolen land, and buried financial records, then Cora had been a liability. But why hide the will in a scarecrow? Why not just destroy it?

Unless he didn't know it had been hidden.

Unless... someone else had moved it.

Someone who wanted Hazel to find it.

Hazel sat up in bed, heart skipping.

What if the scarecrow wasn't a warning?

What if it was a message?

A breadcrumb trail left by someone *else* who knew the truth?

Someone who wasn't trying to stop her at all.

Someone who was trying to help.

Trick or Trap

Halloween Eve arrived draped in silver fog and the scent of woodsmoke.

Wicker's Hollow glowed beneath strings of flickering orange lights. The barn—cleaned, swept, and suspiciously cheerful-looking—had been transformed for the town's annual **Masquerade Ball**, the crown jewel of the Harvest Moon Festival. But behind the caramel apples and dancing scarecrows, behind the glittering masks and sugary smiles, a noose was quietly tightening.

And Hazel Greene was holding the rope.

She stood just inside the barn doors, dressed in a simple black velvet gown, a raven-feathered mask perched over her eyes. In her gloved hand, she clutched a folded sheet of aged paper—**the bait**.

The fake blackmail letter had been Tilly's idea. Crafted with expert flair and a little dramatic flair ("Cora would've written it in lipstick if she could," Tilly had said), it threatened to expose the mayor's embezzlement and referenced the missing will... with just enough detail to make it look like the real thing.

Hazel had left it in the mayor's mailbox. No signature. No warning. Just a single word written at the bottom: **Soon.**

Now, she waited.

Guests flooded into the barn in a swirl of masks, velvet, and glitter.

There was laughter. Music. Bowls of punch that would stain your soul orange. But Hazel was watching the *faces* behind the masks.

Mayor Pickens arrived late. His usually smug posture had shifted into something tighter, tenser. He clutched a tumbler of cider like it might explode. His eyes scanned the room, never quite meeting anyone's.

Ned Wicker lingered in a corner, nursing a drink. Caleb hovered near the dance floor, glancing up every few minutes like he was waiting for something—or someone—to appear.

Sheriff Marsh entered last, nodding once at Hazel. He was here at her request, hidden in plain sight, with instructions to stay back unless someone screamed—or ran.

Hazel moved through the crowd, the fake letter tucked inside her pocket, her pulse syncing with the violin music.

She didn't have to wait long.

The mayor approached her near the dessert table, where ghost cupcakes were lined up like sugar-sweet sentries.

"Lovely party," he said tightly.

Hazel smiled beneath her mask. "Almost… theatrical."

Pickens' jaw twitched.

"You seem tense," she added. "Did you lose something?"

"I think you and I need to talk."

"Do we?" Hazel stepped closer. "Or are you going to offer me hush money in pumpkin scones?"

His face went pale.

Hazel reached into her pocket and pulled out the folded paper.

Pickens stiffened. "What is that?"

She held it just out of his reach.

"I think you know."

Pickens lunged.

Hazel stepped back just as a flash went off—Tilly, perched by the drink table, had snapped a photo on her phone.

The crowd hushed. Sheriff Marsh moved through the barn like a storm cloud.

The mayor froze, caught between outrage and terror.

"It's not what you think," he said quickly. "I didn't kill her. I swear.

I—I just—she found out about the land deal. About the money. But I never touched her. I told her to keep quiet and she laughed in my face. Said she had the will somewhere safe. I thought she was bluffing—"

"Then why did you try to steal it from the barn?" Hazel asked, loud enough for the room to hear.

Pickens swallowed. "Because I thought maybe Ned had it."

"You own the barn."

He looked around, eyes wild now. "That doesn't mean—"

"Then why did you break into the library?"

Pickens froze.

Hazel let the silence do the rest.

Marsh stepped forward. "We'll need you to come with us, Harold."

But Hazel wasn't watching him anymore.

She was watching **Caleb**, who had gone perfectly still by the barn doors.

He wasn't relieved. He wasn't even surprised.

He looked... disappointed.

And then he turned and walked out into the night.

Hazel followed.

Outside, the air was colder. Crisper. Moonlight spilled like silver across the grass.

She found Caleb near the pumpkin patch, leaning against the fence, hands shoved in his pockets.

"You knew," Hazel said quietly.

He didn't answer.

"She was your mother."

Caleb exhaled. "I didn't know for sure. Not until you showed me that photo in the barn. I thought I was just some hired help Ned took pity on. Then I saw the way he looked at me. The way he *didn't* look at me. And I knew."

"She tried to claim what was hers."

"She tried to claim me." His voice cracked. "And he buried her like a secret."

Hazel stood beside him, the wind curling around them both like a whisper from the grave.

"Did you plant the scarecrow?"

Caleb nodded slowly. "I couldn't protect her. But I could make someone *look*."

They stood in silence as the barn behind them lit up with dancing and cider and sugar-coated ignorance.

Then Caleb said, "You're not done yet, you know."

Hazel raised an eyebrow. "No?"

He turned to her, a faint smile on his lips. "Cora wasn't the only one who knew where the bodies were buried."

Hazel's breath caught.

"Meaning...?"

"Meaning," he said, pushing off the fence and walking into the dark, "you might want to check the orchard next."

The Killer Unmasked

The orchard was silent, save for the slow creak of wind through branches that had long since shed their fruit. The trees stood like bare-boned witnesses, gnarled and ancient, their roots hidden beneath frost-bitten soil and fallen leaves. Hazel's boots crunched as she stepped deeper between the rows, guided by a dim flashlight beam and the unmistakable sense that something was about to end.

She found Caleb at the edge of the old stone wall that bordered Wicker's Hollow, standing beneath a crooked apple tree, the only one that still had a single withered fruit dangling from a high branch. He looked oddly peaceful there, hands in his coat pockets, staring up at the stars as though waiting for judgment.

"You came," he said softly, without turning.

Hazel took a slow step forward, heart thudding. "You left a trail for me to follow. You wanted me to."

"I wasn't sure you would. But you're... good at puzzles." He finally turned, and even in the moonlight, Hazel could see the weariness in his face. "Smarter than the rest of them. You looked where no one else dared."

"I thought you were trying to help me," she said. "You made me think the mayor was the villain. You fed me the clues. The letters. The scarf. You led me to the scarecrow."

"I did help," Caleb said calmly. "I just didn't tell you what kind of story we were solving."

Hazel's stomach twisted.

"I wanted the truth," he continued. "But not just for me. For her too."

Hazel narrowed her eyes. "Cora?"

Caleb nodded once. "She was the beginning of all of this. The lies. The power games. The secrets. She destroyed lives. Then laughed like it was nothing."

"She was your mother."

"Barely." His tone sharpened, the softness gone now. "You think blood means something? I begged her to acknowledge me. For years. And when I finally got back here, when I found her, when I told her I knew everything—she mocked me. Said I'd never be a Wicker. Said I was just a mistake she buried like the others."

Hazel's fingers tightened around the flashlight. "What others?"

"She had enemies. Secrets. Lovers. She ruined people with a smirk. And then she acted like she was untouchable."

"You killed her."

"I gave her a stage," he said. "That's what she would've wanted. Center of attention. A twisted harvest queen, displayed for all to see."

He reached into his coat pocket and pulled out a small object—a **golden apple charm**.

"You left this in the library," Hazel said.

"I wanted you to find it. I wanted you to *see*. What she did. What they all did."

Hazel took a step back, toward the harvest table behind her, laden with centerpieces and leftover decorations from the festival. Her heart thundered as Caleb's voice dropped to a whisper.

"You were supposed to expose them all," he said. "Ned. The mayor. Sheriff Marsh. All of them complicit. All of them let her twist this town into knots. But you got too close."

He stepped forward now.

"And now you have a choice."

Hazel's voice was steady. "What choice?"

"You can bury the rest. Or join her."

Hazel moved fast.

She turned, grabbed the nearest object—a **decorative gourd**, painted gold—and hurled it toward Caleb's head. It hit with a dull *crack*, knocking him sideways. He stumbled, growling, and lunged toward her—but by then, she was already yelling.

"NOW!"

From the shadows, Sheriff Marsh emerged, gun drawn, flashlight beam slicing through the night like lightning. "Drop it, Caleb!"

But Caleb didn't listen. He lunged again, grabbing Hazel's arm and trying to drag her down. She fought back, jabbing him in the ribs with her elbow, twisting free. The two of them tumbled into the leaf-strewn orchard floor, grappling among roots and damp earth.

Marsh tackled Caleb from behind, yanking him off Hazel and slamming him to the ground. "That's enough!" he barked, cuffing him with a practiced snap. "It's over."

Caleb didn't fight. He just lay there, panting, smiling faintly at Hazel through bloodied lips.

"She was rotten," he whispered. "Rotten to the core. I just carved her true."

Hazel sat back on her heels, catching her breath, arms trembling from adrenaline and cold.

Marsh looked at her. "You okay?"

She nodded, barely. "I am now."

They walked Caleb to the waiting cruiser. The town was still. No music. No laughter. Only the quiet crunch of leaves and the occasional crow cawing from somewhere high above.

It was nearly 3 a.m. by the time Hazel returned to the library. She walked through the stacks in silence, running her fingers along the spines of books like they were old friends. In the reading nook, a jack-o'-lantern still flickered. She sat beside it, still in her masquerade gown, now scuffed and torn.

Tilly arrived ten minutes later, holding two coffees and a bag of scones. She didn't say anything as she slid into the chair across from her.

Hazel took the coffee gratefully and looked out the window.

"So," Tilly said after a moment. "Is this how all your storytimes end?"

Hazel gave a small, tired laugh. "Only the ones with murder, betrayal, and a gourd-based weapon."

Tilly leaned forward, lowering her voice. "So, what happens now?"

Hazel looked out toward the darkened town square, where autumn decorations still fluttered in the breeze like nothing had happened.

"Now?" she said. "Now I go back to work."

"And the mystery?"

Hazel picked up the golden apple charm, now resting on the windowsill.

"Oh, that's already written."

Tilly raised a brow. "What's the title?"

Hazel smiled faintly, eyes twinkling.

"*The Pumpkin Patch Murders.*"

Falling Leaves and Fresh Starts

A week later, Autumnboro looked like something out of a painting.

The maple trees had hit peak color—bold reds, golden yellows, and rich russets swirling across Main Street like confetti. Scarecrows still stood sentry at every storefront, and the scent of cider hung in the air long after the last cup had been poured at the Harvest Moon Festival.

But for once, Hazel Greene wasn't chasing clues. She wasn't interviewing suspects or digging up secrets beneath gravestones. Today, she was just... being.

Which, it turned out, was harder than it looked.

"You're fidgeting again," Tilly said, sliding a warm dish of butternut squash lasagna onto the table. "That's your thinking-about-murder face."

Hazel gave her a wry smile. "That obvious?"

"Only to people who've seen you use a gourd as a self-defense weapon."

They sat in Tilly's sunlit kitchen, the windows cracked open to let the crisp October air drift in. On the table: candles, pie, a pot of spiced apple tea, and enough cozy food to feed the entire book club. Hazel took a deep breath and let it all soak in.

"It's just weird," she admitted. "A week ago I was crawling through a corn maze, reading blackmail letters in a barn, and now people are thanking me with baked goods and hugs."

"Well," Tilly said, handing her a slice of pumpkin cheesecake, "you did solve a murder. That buys you at least two months of casseroles and very awkward small talk."

Hazel laughed. "One woman called me 'our own Miss Marple but with better hair.'"

"She's not wrong."

There was a knock at the front door. Tilly peeked through the curtain, smirked, and opened it.

"Afternoon, Sheriff."

Eli Marsh stood on the porch, a fresh-pressed shirt beneath his brown jacket, a slight shift in his usual no-nonsense demeanor. He held two takeaway cups of coffee and a folded newspaper tucked under one arm.

"I come bearing caffeine," he said. "And a proposition."

Tilly raised an eyebrow. "Is this the kind of proposition I should leave the room for?"

"Probably," he replied with a smirk, handing Hazel the coffee. "But first, this is for you."

He handed her the newspaper, folded to the editorial section.

Hazel's eyes widened.

At the top of the page:

"Library Files: Notes From Autumnboro's Own Amateur Sleuth"

by Hazel Greene

"Mayor Pickens stepped down this morning," Eli said. "Turns out blackmail and embezzlement don't mix well with small-town politics. The *Gazette* needs new columnists, and the editor liked the way you think. She wants you writing a regular mystery piece."

Hazel blinked. "I... really?"

"Really." He sipped his coffee. "And I think it's good for you. You've got a nose for trouble. Might as well use it legally."

Tilly leaned against the doorway, arms crossed and smiling like a proud big sister.

"So what do you say, Hazel?" she asked. "Ready to be Autumnboro's official mystery magnet?"

Hazel looked down at the paper. Her name in print. Her voice on the page. It was surreal.

"I say," she said, "I've already got the next title in mind."

"Oh?" Eli asked, brow raised. "Do I need to be worried?"

She smiled, sipping her coffee. "Let's just say there's something weird going on at the antique shop."

Eli groaned. "You're going to make me do paperwork, aren't you?"

"Probably."

Tilly slipped back into the kitchen. "Well, if you're going to start another investigation, I suggest you both finish your pie first."

Hazel caught Eli's gaze and saw something warm behind it—something promising. He sat beside her, a little closer than necessary, their shoulders almost touching.

Outside, the leaves danced across the sidewalk. The pumpkins on every porch glowed soft and orange. Somewhere down the street, someone was playing old jazz on a record player loud enough for it to drift on the wind.

Hazel looked out at her town—the town she knew better now than ever before—and smiled.

Cora Belle might be gone, her secrets buried with her, but Autumnboro had plenty more where that came from.

And Hazel Greene was ready for every last one.

THE END
(for now...)

www.ingramcontent.com/pod-product-compliance
Lightning Source LLC
LaVergne TN
LVHW020443080526
838202LV00055B/5329